ZONDERKIDZ

The Berenstain Bears® Show God's Love
Copyright © 2010 by Berenstain Bears, Inc.
Illustrations © 2010 by Berenstain Bears, Inc.

Requests for information should be addressed to:
Zonderkidz, *Grand Rapids, Michigan 49530*

ISBN 978-0-310-72010-2

The Berenstain Bears® Love Their Neighbors ISBN 9780310712497 (2009)
The Berenstain Bears® Play a Good Game ISBN 9780310712527 (2009)
The Berenstain Bears® and a Job Well Done ISBN 9780310712541 (2010)
The Berenstain Bears® Faithful Friends ISBN 9780310712534 (2009)
The Berenstain Bears® and the Gift of Courage ISBN 9780310712565 (2010)

Editor: Mary Hassinger
Cover and interior design: Cindy Davis

Printed in China

10 11 12 13 14 15 /LPC/ 10 9 8 7 6 5 4 3 2 1

The Berenstain Bears®

SHOW GOD'S LOVE

written by Jan and Mike Berenstain

ZONDERVAN.com/
AUTHORTRACKER
follow your favorite authors

ZONDERkidz

Living
Lights™

The Berenstain Bears. love Their Neighbors

written by Jan and Mike Berenstain

ZONDERVAN.com/
AUTHORTRACKER
follow your favorite authors

ZONDERkidz

Living Lights™

"Love your neighbor as yourself."
"And who is my neighbor?"
—Luke 10:27-29

The Bear family was quite proud of their handsome tree house home, and they worked hard to keep it neat and tidy. The trim was freshly painted, the front steps were scrubbed, and the windows were washed. The lawn was mowed, and the flower beds were weeded. Even the leaves of the tree were carefully trimmed and clipped.

Most of their neighbors took good care of their homes as well. The Pandas across the street were even bigger neatniks than the Bears. It seemed they were always hard at work sweeping and cleaning.

Farmer Ben's farm just down the road was always in apple-pie order too. Even his chicken coop was as neat as a pin. "A place for everything and everything in its place, that's my motto," said Farmer Ben.

The Bear family had a few neighbors whose houses were positively fancy—like Mayor Honeypot, the bear who rode around Bear Town in his long lavender limousine. His house was three stories tall and built of brick. It had a big brass knocker on the front door and statues of flamingos on the front lawn.

Even more impressive was the mansion of Squire Grizzly, the richest bear in all Bear Country. It stood on a hill surrounded by acres of lawns and gardens. Dozens of servants and gardeners took care of the place.

The Bear family was proud of their neighborhood, and they got along well with all their neighbors.

Except for the Bogg brothers.

The Bogg brothers lived in a run-down old shack not far from the Bear family's tree house—but what a difference! Their roof was caving in, and the whole place leaned to one side. There was junk all over the yard. Chickens, dogs, and cats ran everywhere. A big pig wallowed in the mud out back.

"Those Bogg brothers!" Mama would say whenever she saw them. "They're a disgrace to the neighborhood!"

"Yes," agreed Papa, "they certainly are a problem."

One bright spring morning, the Bear family was working outside, cleaning up and fixing up, when the Bogg brothers came along. They were driving their broken-down old jalopy. It made a terrific clanking racket.

As they drove past the tree house, one of the Bogg brothers spit out of the car. It narrowly missed the Bears' mailbox.

"Really!" said Mama, shocked. "Those Bogg brothers are a disgrace!"

"I agree," said Papa, getting the mail out of the mailbox. "I'm afraid they're not very good neighbors."

Papa looked through the mail and found a big yellow flier rolled up. He opened it and showed it to the rest of the family.

COME ONE! COME ALL!
To the
BIG BEAR TOWN FESTIVAL
Help celebrate our
wonderful neighborhood.
= Games, rides, contests, prizes =
☆ FIREWORKS! ☆
Saturday, 9 AM to 9 PM
Horace J. Honeypot, Mayor

"Oh, boy!" said Sister and Brother. "It's like a big block party! Can we go?"
"It certainly sounds like fun," said Mama. "What do you think, Papa?"
"Everyone in town will be there," said Papa. "We ought to go too."
"Yea!" cried the cubs.

So, on Saturday morning, they all piled into the car. They had a picnic basket and folding chairs. They were looking forward to a day of fun and excitement.

But, as they drove along, the car began to make a funny sound. It started out as a Pocketa-pocketa-pocketa! But it soon developed into a Pocketa-WHEEZE! Pocketa-WHEEZE!

POCKETA-POCKETA-POCKETA-WHEEEZE!-POCKETA-WHEEEEZE!

"Oh, dear!" said Mama. "What is that awful sound the car is making?"
Just then, the car made a much worse sound—a loud CLUNK! It came to a sudden halt, and the radiator cap blew off. They all climbed out, and Papa opened the hood.

"I guess it's overheated," said Papa, waving at the cloud of steam with his hat.

"Oh, no!" said Sister. "How are we going to get to the Bear Town Festival?"

"Maybe someone will stop and give us a hand," said Papa hopefully. "Look, here comes a car. Let's all wave. Maybe they will stop."

It was Mayor and Mrs. Honeypot in their long lavender limousine. They were on their way to the festival too. Their car slowed down, but it didn't stop. The mayor leaned his head out of the window.

"Sorry, we can't stop!" he said. "We're late already. I'm Master of Ceremonies today. I've got to be there on time. I'm sure someone will stop to help you."

And he pulled away with a squeal of tires.

"Hmm!" said Papa. "Maybe someone else will come along."

Soon, another car did come along. It was Squire and Lady Grizzly being driven to the festival in their big black Grizz-Royce. They slowed down too. Lady Grizzly rolled down her window.

"I'm afraid we can't stop," she said. "We don't have time. I am the judge of the flower-arranging contest. We simply must hurry."

And with that, they pulled away.

"Maybe no one is going to stop," said Sister. "Maybe we're never going get to the festival."

"One of our neighbors is sure to stop and help us," said Mama. "After all, that's what neighbors are for."

"Yeah," said Brother. "But do *they* know that?"

A cloud of dust appeared down the road.

"Here comes someone now!" Sister said eagerly.

The dust cloud drew closer, and they could hear a clackety racket getting louder.

"Uh-oh!" said Papa, shading his eyes and peering down the road. "If that's who I think it is …"

It was!

It was the Bogg brothers. They came clanking up in their rickety old jalopy and screeched to a halt. First one, then another, then another of the Bogg brothers came climbing out.

"Howdy!" said the first Bogg brother.

"Hello, there," said Papa.

"I'm Lem," said the first Bogg brother. "I can see yer havin' some trouble with your ve-hicle."

"Well, yes, we are," said Papa.

"Maybe we can give you a hand," said Lem.

"That would be very neighborly of you," said Papa.

"Hey, Clem! Hey, Shem!" called Lem. "Git out the rope!"

The other two Bogg brothers rooted around in the back of the jalopy and came up with a length of rope. They hitched it to the back bumper of their car and tied the other end around the front bumper of the Bears' car.

"All aboard!" said Lem. The Bear family climbed hastily back in their car. The Bogg brothers pulled away, towing the Bears' car behind them.

"Where are they taking us?" asked Mama.

Papa shrugged. "At least we're moving!"

Brother and Sister hoped the Bogg brothers weren't taking them down to their old shack. They didn't want to meet that big pig.

They soon pulled into a run-down old filling station. Someone who looked like an older version of the Bogg brothers came out.

"Hello, Uncle Zeke," said Lem.

"Hello, Nephew," said Uncle Zeke. "What can I do you fer?"

"These poor folks broke down on the road," said Lem. "You reckon you can fix them up?"

"Let's take a look," said Uncle Zeke.

He looked under the car's hood, banged and clanged around, and came up with a length of burst hose.

"Radee-ator hose," he said. "Busted clean open. I should have another one of them around here somewheres."

Uncle Zeke rummaged around behind the filling station and soon came back with a radiator hose. He banged and clanged under the hood for a few more minutes.

"There," he said, wiping his hands. "Good as new. We'll top off the radee-ator, and you folks can be on your way."

"Thank you very much!" said Papa, relieved. He shook hands with Uncle Zeke and the Bogg brothers.

"Thank you!" said Mama, Brother, and Sister. Honey Bear waved. "How much do we owe you?" asked Papa, reaching for his wallet. "Nothin'," said Lem. "This one is on us. After all, we're neighbors."

"That's right," said Mama with a gulp. "We are. In fact, how would you neighbors like to come over to our house for dinner next week?"

Papa, Brother, and Sister all stared at Mama with their mouths open.

"That's right neighborly of you," said Lem. "Don't mind if we do! Shem's cookin' has been getting a bit tiresome—too much possum stew."

"We were on our way to the Bear Town Festival," said Papa. "Would you like to join us?"

"Sure would!" said Lem. "We ain't been to a big shindig since Grandpap's ninetieth birthday party!"

So, the Bear family drove to Bear Town with the Bogg brothers and Uncle Zeke.

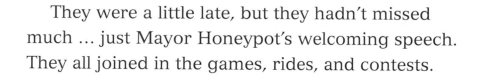

They were a little late, but they hadn't missed much … just Mayor Honeypot's welcoming speech. They all joined in the games, rides, and contests.

When it was time for the fireworks, the Bogg brothers livened things up with some music of their own.

The next week, the Bogg brothers came over to the Bears' tree house for dinner. They wore their best clothes and got all spruced up for the occasion. They even brought a housewarming gift: a big pot of Shem's special possum stew.

It was delicious!

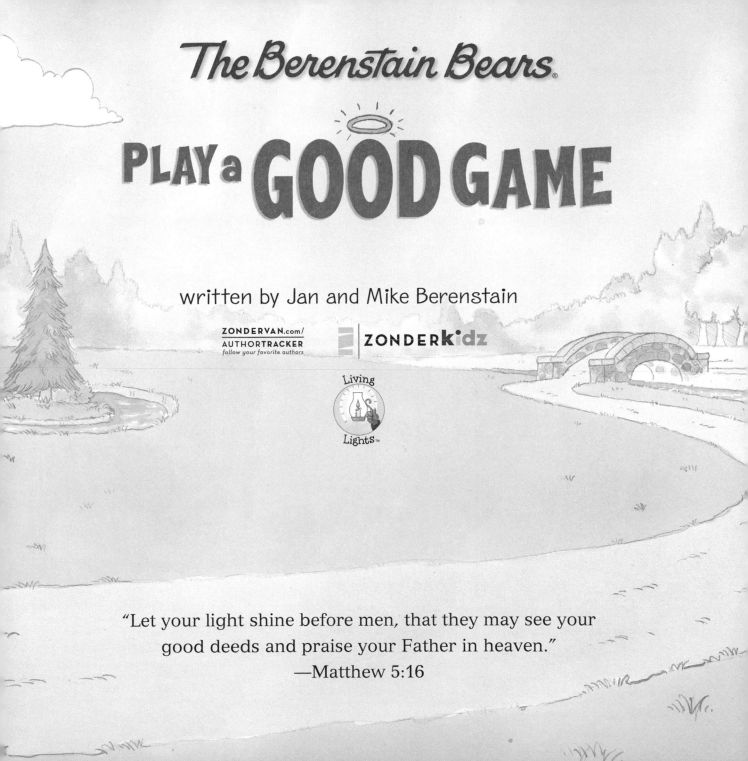

The Berenstain Bears®

PLAY a GOOD GAME

written by Jan and Mike Berenstain

ZONDERVAN.com/
AUTHORTRACKER
follow your favorite authors

ZONDERkidz

Living
Lights™

"Let your light shine before men, that they may see your
good deeds and praise your Father in heaven."
—Matthew 5:16

Brother and Sister Bear loved all kinds of sports. They played one sport or another all the year round.

But in the fall, when the leaves turned color and the first frosty nip was in the air, the thoughts of Brother and Sister Bear turned to … soccer! They dusted off the old soccer ball and headed for the soccer field.

Their team was called the Rockets, and they did rocket around the field. They weren't the best team in the league, but they were pretty good.

Their coach was none other than Brother and Sister's own Papa Bear. He didn't really[2] know that much about soccer. But he tried hard and was very good at cheering them on.

Brother and Sister tried hard too. The best players on the team were the Brunowsky twins, Bram and Bam. But Brother and Sister had their strong points.

Brother was a left-footed kicker. He was given the job of corner kicks from the right side. He was great at "bending" the ball in toward the goal.

Sister was a skillful "header." She could bop Brother's kicks right into the net with her head.

"My head is like a rock!" she said, rapping the top of her head with her knuckles.

"It sure is!" agreed Brother.

"Hey!" said Sister.

Brother and Sister didn't worry too much about winning. It was fun just to get out there and play.

"Remember, team," Papa always told them, "it's not whether you win or lose that counts, but how you play the game!"

There was one team, though, that didn't feel that way—the Steamrollers. Their best players were Too-Tall Grizzly and his gang. They were the schoolyard bullies of Bear Country, and they were big and tough and strong. They weren't very good soccer players, but that didn't matter. If you got in their way, they just ran over you.

Their coach was Too-Tall's dad, Two-Ton Grizzly. He was just as rough and tough as his son, only a whole lot bigger.

He said, "It isn't how you play the game that counts, but whether you win or lose!"

The Rockets' first game of the season was against the Steamrollers. Brother and Sister were definitely not looking forward to it.

"Don't worry," Coach Papa told his team. "Just play your best, and you'll all do fine!"

The players' families were in the stands to see the first game. Mama Bear was there with Honey Bear, of course. Grizzly Gramps and Gran were there too. Gramps was already whistling and cheering and stamping his feet.

"Come on, Rockets!" he yelled and, putting two fingers in his mouth, blew a whistle that you could have heard all over Bear Country.

"Now, Gramps!" said Gran. "Please control yourself."

"Aw, shucks!" he said. "Makin' a big fuss at a ball game is half the fun of rootin' for your team. It's all in good fun."

Brother and Sister were surprised to see that their Sunday school teacher, Missus Ursula, was in the stands. Missus Ursula had been the Sunday school teacher in Bear Country for a long, long time. She'd even taught Mama and Papa Bear when they were cubs.

Then, Brother and Sister remembered that Missus Ursula was the Brunowsky twins' grandmother. Bram and Bam waved to her as they ran onto the field.

The families of the Steamrollers were in the stands too. There was
Too-Tall's mother, Too-Too Grizzly, and his big sister, Too-Much. Too-Much
really was a big sister—she was almost twice Too-Tall's height. When she
saw Brother, she waved and fluttered her eyelashes. She had a little crush on
Brother. Brother just blushed.

The Steamrollers ran onto the field to warm up. They looked huge!

Brother and Sister looked at each other. They were going to get clobbered! Even Bram and Bam looked a little worried.

The referee blew his whistle, and the game began.

The Rockets had the ball, and Bram and Bam quickly brought it down the field, passing it expertly back and forth. Bram took the ball and headed for the goal.

"TAKE HIM OUT!" yelled
Two-Ton from the sidelines.
Too-Tall came charging in like a water
buffalo, slide-tackled Bram, and stole the
ball. Bram went flying head over heels.

"Foul!" yelled Coach Papa.

But the referee shook his head. "He was going for the ball—no foul!"

"Going for the ball!" muttered Papa under his breath. "He was going for the ball right through my player!"

Too-Tall and his
gang hustled the ball down
the field and quickly scored a
goal.

"How you like that one, shorty?"
Too-Tall sneered at Bram as he
trotted off the field.

"That's enough of that!" said the referee.
"Play soccer!"

"Talk about poor sportsmanship!"
muttered Papa.

The Rockets had the ball again. But the same thing happened. The Steamrollers just steamrollered them, scoring one goal after another. At halftime, the score was Steamrollers, five; Rockets, zero.

Steamrollers	Rockets
05	00

Coach Papa gave them a pep talk. "Don't let it get you down!" said Papa. "You're playing a good, clean game! The Steamrollers don't play fair. All they're interested in is winning, and they don't care how they do it. You wouldn't want to win that way, would you?"

"No," said Bram.

"But," said Bam, "it would be nice to score just one goal."

"I know how!" said Brother,
getting an idea. "Let's set up a corner kick."
"Yeah!" said Sister. "They don't
know that Brother kicks left footed.
Maybe we can fool them!"

So the Rockets tried
it. The next time they
had the ball, Bam
kicked it off Too-Tall's
leg on purpose, and
it went out of bounds.
That set up the corner
kick.

Carefully, Brother placed the ball in the right corner and kicked it hard with his left foot. The ball curved beautifully. Sister was right there. She leaped straight up, tipped her head, and bopped the ball into the goal! The score was now five to one.

But as Sister came down, Too-Tall charged her. He plowed into her and knocked her flat. Sister saw stars circling around her head and heard little birds chirping.

"Wha' happened?" she asked.

"Too-Tall happened!" said Brother, helping her up. "Are you okay?"

"I think so," said Sister, standing up. "Yeah, I'm all in one piece." Sister was a tough little cub.

Brother looked around for Too-Tall. He was so mad he was going to run right through him. But the referee had Too-Tall over to one side and was handing him a red card. Too-Tall was getting thrown out of the game for unnecessary roughness.

"WHAD'YA MEAN—UNNECESSARY ROUGHNESS?" bellowed Coach Two-Ton, running out onto the field.

Two-Ton and the referee stood nose-to-nose, hollering at each other.

"Uh-oh!" said Brother. "Here comes Papa!"
Coach Papa came running onto the field too.
"That was my daughter who got unnecessarily roughed, you big lummox!" he yelled at Two-Ton. Now the referee was trying to keep them apart.

The stands emptied. Everyone ran onto the field. The players watched in amazement as Mama and Grizzly Gramps and Gram tried to drag Papa away while Too-Too and Too-Much Grizzly tried to hold Two-Ton back. Everyone was shouting and shoving and name-calling.

That's when a slim, slightly bent figure walked slowly onto the field. The crowd quieted down. A few of them took off their hats.

It was their Sunday school teacher, Missus Ursula.

"Now, Papa Bear," she said sternly. "And you too, Two-Ton Grizzly."

"Yes, Missus Ursula?" they said meekly.

"I'm very disappointed with both of you," she said, shaking her head. "Is this the way I taught you to behave in my Sunday school?"

"No, Missus Ursula," mumbled both coaches, hanging their heads.

"Is this any sort of example to set for the cubs?" she asked.

"No, Missus Ursula," they said.

"Well, then," she said. "Remember, 'Blessed are the peacemakers, for they will be called sons of God.' Now, let's see you two shake hands and finish the game."

So Papa and Two-Ton shook hands. Everyone took their seats, the referee blew his whistle, and the game went on.

For the rest of the game, no one heard a peep out of Coach Two-Ton or Coach Papa. The Steamrollers scored one more goal, and the Rockets scored two. The final score was six to three. Everyone played fair and had a lot of fun … whether they won or lost.

Steamrollers Rockets
06 03

After the game, both teams got together and went out to dinner at the Burger Bear.

Too-Much Grizzly sat next to Brother and fluttered her eyelashes at him. Brother just blushed and munched away on his double cheeseburger.

The Berenstain Bears and A Job Well Done

written by Jan and Mike Berenstain

"Whatever your hand finds to do,
do it with all your might."
—Ecclesiastes 9:10

ZONDERVAN.com/
AUTHORTRACKER
follow your favorite authors

ZONDERkidz

Living Lights™

It was spring in Bear Country. And that meant that it was spring cleaning and fix-up time at the Bear family's tree house. Mama, Papa, Brother, Sister, and even Honey all had jobs to do.

Mama and Papa got right down to work. Mama hung up rugs on the line to beat the dirt out of them. Papa started to fix the broken railing on the front steps.

Brother and Sister had a job too. They were supposed to clean up the old playhouse in the backyard. Honey was going to help them.

They all got off to a good start. The sun was shining, and the air was fresh and clean. Birds were singing, and bright flowers were blooming in the garden.

Mama whacked at the rugs. Huge clouds of dirt flew out of them.

Papa's tools were everywhere. He knelt down to carve a piece of
wood into the right shape for the railing.

Brother, Sister, and Honey had everything they needed for their job. They had brooms and brushes, cloths and mops, buckets of hot water and lots of soap. First, they were going to sweep out the inside of the playhouse.

"Uh-oh!" said Brother, looking inside the playhouse. "Spiders!"

Sister and Honey peeked inside. Sure enough, there were some big, hairy spiders sitting in their webs up in the corners of the playhouse. Brother, Sister, and Honey hated spiders!

"Yuck!" they all said.

"What should we do?" asked Sister.

"Let's not sweep out the inside," said Brother. "Let's scrub the outside. Maybe that will scare the spiders out."

That's what they did. Brother worked his way around the playhouse with his scrub brush, whistling while he worked.

"Hey, look!" he said when he got to the back. "We left some baseball stuff out here."

There was an old baseball, a bat, and a glove behind the playhouse.

Brother picked up the ball, tossed it in the air, and caught it. Sister picked up the bat and gave it a few swings.

"Pitch it in!" she said to Brother.

Brother wound up and tossed the ball to Sister. She swatted it across the lawn.

"Here, Honey," said Brother, giving her the glove. "You be the outfielder."

Honey toddled out into the lawn and sat down.

Meanwhile, back at the tree house, Mama and Papa were hard at work. Mama was nearly done with the rugs. She was absolutely covered with dirt.

Papa was nearly finished with the railing. He fastened
the wood in place, then straightened up and stretched.

That's when Papa noticed Honey sitting in the middle of the lawn. He couldn't see Brother or Sister. They were behind the tree house.

"What is Honey doing just sitting there?" wondered Papa.

A baseball came sailing into sight and landed near Honey. She grabbed it and threw it back.

"Hmmm!" said Papa, rubbing his chin.

Papa walked around the tree house and saw Brother and Sister playing baseball. Their brooms, brushes, cloths, and mops were all lying on the ground.

Papa stood behind Brother and Sister.

"Baseball is a fine springtime activity," he said, "but so is spring cleaning!"

Brother and Sister spun around and hid the ball and bat behind their backs.

"Oh, hi, Papa!" they both grinned. "We were just taking a little break."

Papa looked into the very dirty playhouse.

"It looks like you've been taking a *big* break," he said. "You've hardly touched this playhouse."

"But Papa," started Brother.

"There are lots of spiders in there!" finished Sister.

Papa smiled. He remembered how scared he was of spiders when he was a cub. He still didn't like them very much. "Well," he said, "I'll chase the spiders out for you. But, then, you need to get the job done."

Papa chased the spiders out of the playhouse with a broom. They ran off and hid in the storage shed, which was a better home for them, anyway.

Then, Brother, Sister, and Honey went back to work.

"Did you know that the Bible has something to say about working hard and getting the job done?" asked Papa as they cleaned.

"No," said Brother.

"What does it say?" said Sister.

"It says," said Papa, "'finish your outdoor work and get your fields ready; after that, build your house.'"

"Did you build a house today, Papa?" asked Sister.

"Well," said Papa, proudly, "I built a new railing."

"And," added Mama, who had come up to see what was going on, "it says in the Bible that God made work for us to do and there's nothing better than to enjoy your work."

"Did you enjoy your work, Mama?" asked Brother.

Mama rubbed some of the dirt off her face. "Well," she said, "I enjoy my clean rugs—and you will enjoy your clean playhouse."

"Especially without all those spiders!" agreed Sister.
"Yuck!" said Honey.
Mama, Papa, Brother, and Sister all laughed.

The Berenstain Bears®
Faithful Friends

written by Jan and Mike Berenstain

ZONDERVAN.com/
AUTHORTRACKER
follow your favorite authors

ZONDERkidz

"Do not forsake your friend."
—Proverbs 27:10

Lizzy Bruin was Sister Bear's very
best friend. It seemed like they had
been best friends for a very long time.

Lizzy Bruin and Sister Bear had been through a lot together. Once they had a slumber party that got a little out of hand.

They were in the school play that time Brother forgot his lines.

They built their own clubhouse when Brother kept them out of his.

They played dress up
and dolls and rode their
bikes and picked flowers
and rolled down hills and
giggled.

Sister was glad she had such a good friend. She could always rely on Lizzy to be there for her. They hardly ever fought or argued. Not, that is, until Sister started to spend more time with Suzy MacGrizzie.

Suzy was a new cub in town. At first, Sister and her friends didn't pay much attention to Suzy. But then, Sister noticed how lonely Suzy was and invited her to play. From then on, Suzy was part of Sister's little group.

All of Sister's friends, including Lizzy, liked Suzy. She was one more cub to spend time with and enjoy.

But Suzy was a little different from the other cubs. For one thing, she read an awful lot. And she was interested in different things—science, for instance. Suzy invited Sister over one night to look at the sky. Suzy pointed her telescope up at the moon.

"Wow!" said Sister, looking into the eyepiece. "It looks so close." She could actually see mountains and valleys and craters on the moon. It was very interesting.

One day, Suzy asked Sister to go on a butterfly hunt with her. They took butterfly nets and went out into the fields.

Sister caught a big yellow butterfly with black stripes. Suzy caught one that had bright red and blue spots on it and long swallowtails. It was very beautiful. After they studied the butterflies for a while, they let them go, and the butterflies sailed up into the sky over the trees.

"They're so pretty!" said Sister.

On their way back, Suzy and Sister ran into Lizzy and their friends Anna and Millie. They were all carrying their Bearbie dolls.

"Hiya, gang!" called Sister when she saw them. "Suzy and I were out catching butterflies. You should have seen the big yellow one I got!"

"Yeah, great," said Lizzy. "Well, see you, I guess."
"Wait a minute," said Sister. "Where are you all going?"
"We're going over to my garage to play Bearbie dolls," said Lizzy.
"Can Suzy and I come too?" asked Sister.

"It looks like you two are already pretty busy," said Lizzy. "Come on, girls." With that, Lizzy and her friends went on their way.

"How do you like that?" said Sister, hurt and angry. "Who does she think she is? Come on, Suzy, we'll play over at my house. Who needs them, anyway?"

When they got to the Bear family's tree house, Suzy and Sister found Brother Bear and Cousin Fred getting out their fishing tackle.

"Lizzy and your friends were here looking for you," Brother said. "I told them you were playing with Suzy. Lizzy didn't seem very happy."

"That Lizzy Bruin!" said Sister, annoyed. "What business is it of hers who I play with?"

"I guess she's jealous," said Brother.

"Jealous?" said Sister, puzzled.

"Sure," said Brother. "She's been your best friend for years. You mean a lot to her. She's just worried that maybe you don't like her as much as you used to."

"Oh," said Sister, "that's silly!" It was true that she liked her new friend, Suzy. But Lizzy would always be her best friend.

"What should I do?" Sister wondered.

Cousin Fred spoke up. "You know what the Bible says: 'Wounds from a friend can be trusted.'" Fred liked to memorize things.

"Huh?" said both Sister and Brother. "What does that mean?"

Suzy answered—she liked to memorize things too. "I think it means that when a friend who loves you hurts your feelings, you need to find out what is bothering her."

"Yes," Fred nodded. "And the Bible also says that we shouldn't stay angry with our friends. God wants us to make up with them if we have an argument."

"Oh," said Sister, thoughtfully.

"I have an idea," said Brother. "Fred and I were about to go fishing. Why don't we grab some extra fishing gear and go over to Lizzy's? We can see if they would all like to go fishing with us."

"Great!" said Sister. Suzy grinned.

So they all stopped by Lizzy's garage on their way to the fishing hole.

"Hey, Lizzy!" called Sister. "Do you and Anna and Millie want to go fishing with us?"

Lizzy acted like she wasn't so sure. But Anna and Millie were all for it, and Lizzy certainly didn't want to be left out.

Soon, they were all down at the fishing hole. Lizzy cast her line out into the middle of the pond and got her line into a terrible tangle.

"Here, let me help you, Lizzy," said Sister, taking her fishing rod. "I'll untangle it for you."

"Wow, thanks!" said Lizzy. "You're a real friend, Sister."

"I always have been, and I always will be!" said Sister, giving Lizzy a hug.

And together they picked away at the tangled fishing line.

The Berenstain Bears® AND THE GIFT OF COURAGE

written by Jan and Mike Berenstain

ZONDERVAN.com/
AUTHORTRACKER
follow your favorite authors

ZONDERkidz

"Act with courage, and may the Lord be with those who do well."

—2 Chronicles 19:11

Sister loved all animals—not only dogs and cats and birds and bunnies, but lizards and frogs and worms and bugs as well. She knew they were all God's creatures, and she liked to play with them. That's what caused the trouble with Too-Tall.

Too-Tall Grizzly and his gang were the official bullies of Bear Country School. They thought it was fun to push other cubs around, and they had many nasty ways to have fun.

One of their favorites was to bump into a cub on purpose and then make him apologize for being so clumsy.

Of course, they teased anyone anytime about pretty much anything at all. That's what happened to Sister Bear one morning in the school yard.

Sister was standing in line, waiting for the school bell to ring, when a cute little ladybug landed right on her shoulder.

She held out her finger so the ladybug could crawl onto it,
and she chanted a line from an old nursery rhyme.

"Ladybug, ladybug,
fly away home!"

As she watched the ladybug whirr away, Sister heard a nasty voice behind her. It was Too-Tall Grizzly.

"Ladybug, ladybug!" mocked Too-Tall. "Does Sister Bear wuv her wittle wadybug fwends?" he said in a silly, baby-talk voice. The rest of his gang laughed, and quite a few other cubs standing in line laughed with them.

Sister felt so embarrassed she froze. She didn't know what to say or do. She just stood there. Then the school bell rang, and the line began to move. She never got a chance to say or do anything at all.

For the rest of the day, Sister Bear felt terrible. She wished she had stood up against that nasty Too-Tall. She kept thinking of things that she "should have" said. *Maybe,* she thought, *I was just plain scared*! She didn't like the idea of being scared.

By bedtime that evening, Sister had almost stopped worrying about the Too-Tall incident—*almost*. It was Papa Bear's turn to read a bedtime story.

"What will it be tonight?" asked Papa as Brother and Sister snuggled down in their bunk beds.

A thought came into Sister's head. "How about David and Goliath?" she suggested.

"Yes," agreed Brother, "that's a good story."

"All right," said Papa, "David and Goliath it is." He got the *Big Book of Bible Stories* for the cubs down from the bookshelf and settled in to read.

"Long ago in the Holy Land, there lived a young shepherd named David. It was his job to watch over his father's flock of sheep. He knew that God was with him, so he was not afraid of wolves or lions.

"When wolves came sneaking up to the flock, David drove them away with stones from his sling.

"In those days, a giant warrior named Goliath was threatening those who lived in the Holy Land. Goliath towered over all other warriors. No one was brave enough to fight him.

"David heard about Goliath, but David was not afraid. He knew that God was watching over him. So he took some stones and his sling and went out against Goliath.

"When Goliath saw David, he laughed because David was only a boy. He raised his great spear to throw it at David.

"But David quickly put a stone in his sling and swung it around and around his head.

"He let it fly, and it struck Goliath right in the middle of his forehead. Goliath fell to the ground with a crash that shook the earth.

"Little David had struck down the giant warrior! With God's help, David had shown great courage and saved the land from Goliath."

The story was done, and Papa
tucked Brother and Sister into bed.

"David was very brave, wasn't he?"
asked Brother as Papa kissed them
good night.

"He had the bravest heart of all,"
nodded Papa. "You know what they
say, 'Little David was small—but, *oh,
my!*'"

"I don't think I'm brave enough to stand up to someone so much bigger than I am," said Sister. "I would probably be too scared to even move."

"I don't know about that," said Papa, turning out the light. "I think both of you can be quite brave when you need to be. And remember, God is watching over you just like David. That will give you courage."

Brother and Sister fell asleep dreaming about the bravery of young David.

The next morning, Brother and Sister set off for school bright and early. As they strolled along the road, they heard laughing and shouting up ahead. They rounded a bend and saw Too-Tall Grizzly and his gang.

"I wonder what they're up to," said Brother.

"No good, I'll bet," said Sister.

As they came closer, they saw that the gang was throwing rocks up into a tree.

"What's going on, Too-Tall?" asked Brother.

"You're just in time for some fun!"
Too-Tall laughed. "See that hornets'
nest up there?" He pointed at a huge
round nest hanging high in the tree.
"We're going to knock it down and
see what happens."

"Don't do that!" said Sister. "That nest is the hornets' home. If you knock it down, they'll have no place to live."

"Aaaw!" sneered Too-Tall. "Are those hornets more of your wittle buggy fwends? Why don't you 'fly away' and mind your own business?"

While the gang laughed, Too-Tall drew back his arm to hurl a big rock at the nest. But Sister grabbed onto his arm.

"Hey, you little squirt!" yelled Too-Tall. "Let go!"

The rest of the gang charged at Sister to pull her away, but Brother
stepped right in front of them. He glared at them. They didn't like the
look in his eyes but Brother didn't seem the least bit afraid. They all
backed away.

Too-Tall swung Sister around and around like David with his sling. But Sister hung on for all she was worth. Finally, Too-Tall gave a great heave and broke Sister's grip. The rock flew out of his hand and sailed up into the tree. It smacked right into the hornets' nest and knocked it open. A big cloud of angry hornets flew out.

Brother and Sister ducked under some bushes. The hornets bunched themselves up into an angry black ball and headed down after Too-Tall and his gang.

"Yeow!" yelled Too-Tall. "Look out!"

"Run!" yelled the gang.

When they were gone, Brother and Sister peeked out from behind the tree.

"That was close!" said Brother.

"Do you think God was watching over us?" wondered Sister.

"No doubt about it!" nodded Brother. With a sigh of relief, they continued on their way to school.

"You were very brave," said Brother, "going after Too-Tall that way. 'Little Sister was small—but, *oh my!*'"

Sister laughed. "You were pretty brave yourself, standing up to the whole gang that way."

"I guess Papa was right," said Brother. "Even young cubs like us can be brave when we need to be."

"Too-Tall wasn't very brave," said Sister.

"Let's be fair," said Brother. "No one is very brave when it comes to angry hornets."

"No doubt about it!" agreed Sister,
and they walked on to school, arm in arm.

The Berenstain Bears love Their Neighbors

Activities and Questions from Brother and Sister Bear

Talk about it:

1. How does the Bear family feel about the Bogg brothers? Do you think the brothers are easy to like?

2. How did the Bear family show their love for their neighbors?

3. How have you shown love for your neighbors?

Get out and do it:

1. Design a fun car with no top.

2. With your family, help a neighbor with a job like yard work.

3. Write three things you can do to help at home.

The Berenstain Bears.

PLAY a GOOD GAME

Activities and Questions from Brother and Sister Bear

Talk about it:

1. Do you think Brother bear played fair? What could he have done differently to please God?

2. How do you feel when someone else does not play fair?

Get out and do it:

1. Play a team game with your friends: tag, soccer, red rover, or baseball.

2. Design a team logo for a sports team, school, club, or church group.

3. The Steamrollers is a good name for Too-Tall's team. It fits how they play. Come up with a team name that fits how you play a game of your choice.

Activities and Questions from Brother and Sister Bear

Talk about it:

1. Do you have at-home jobs that need to get done before you can have some fun? Name some of the chores you do and how it helps the family when you finish them completely.

2. What do you think Papa Bear meant when he said the Bible says, "finish your outdoor work and get your fields ready; after that, build your house?"

Get out and do it:

1. Design a family chore chart. Hang the chart up and check it daily, making sure you are completing your family responsibilities.

2. Help someone in your family with one of their given jobs around the house. Do not wait to be asked.

Faithful Friends

Activities and Questions from Brother and Sister Bear

Talk about it:

1. How can you invite new friends into your friend group?

2. Have you ever felt left out by a friend? What do you think God would want you to do when that happens?

3. Do you like to do different things with different friends? Name some things you do differently.

Get out and do it:

1. Design a constellation—a group of stars that make a picture. Tape a piece of black paper over the end of an empty toilet paper tube. Use a pin to poke holes in the paper in a design. Look through the tube at a light to see your constellation design.

2. Play Follow the Leader. Take turns being the leader.

The Berenstain Bears
AND THE GIFT OF COURAGE

Activities and Questions from Brother and Sister Bear

Talk about it:

1. What does it mean to be a bully?

2. Have you ever had to stand up to someone who is a bully? What would God want you to do if you met a bully?

3. How can you be brave when you meet someone who is not so nice?

Get out and do it:

1. Draw two barbells on heavy paper or cardboard and cut them out. Write the following words on the barbells and then hang them up in your room to remind you how to act when you feel threatened: Strong at Heart, Strong in Mind.

2. Design a card to give to someone who you believe is brave. Tell that person how much you admire his courage.

"Be loving in everything you do."

—1 Corinthians 16:14 (NIrV)